WIND, RAIN AND SNOW

WIND, RAIN AND SNOW

Written by

Rabia Yıldırım

Published by Tughra Books
345 Clifton Ave., Clifton,
NJ, 07011, USA

www.tughrabooks.com

WIND, RAIN AND SNOW
Project Editor: Betül Ertekin
Translated by Kemal Aydın and Ogulgozel Atakova
Graphic Design: İbrahim Akdağ

ISBN: 978-1-59784-284-6

Printed by
Görsel Dizayn Ofset, Istanbul - TURKEY

CONTENTS

THE STRONG WIND

Wooo! Wooo! That was the sound of the wind. It sounded as if it came from a vacuum cleaner. It was sweeping away everything around.

Sometimes the wind blew mild air, and sometimes cold. Today it was a mild wind. Trees and flowers were gently waving to the right and left.

7

Meanwhile, the winds of the sky were having a conversation:

"This time I am going to break down all these trees by blowing very strongly," one of them said.

"That is not for you to decide," said the other winds. "We have to blow in the way that Almighty Allah wants us to. And even then, our duty is not to harm the environment."

The Strong Wind asked, "All right, then! What is our duty?"

"Of course, first of all, we should set the clouds in motion. And then we should bring together rain clouds so that it can rain," replied the other winds.

Then they went on. "Besides that, we should help bring about further fruit growth by scattering flower seeds. But, it's sunny today. So, today's duty is to cool all living beings. Let's turn to our work right away!"

So, that day only mild winds blew. This made all living beings happy—people, animals and plants. It was very hot in the summer and everyone was trying to cool down.

After the summer, the autumn came. In that season of year strong winds start blowing again. By the winds, trees and animals are informed of the coming winter. So everyone was ready for those strong winds beforehand.

After a while, the roofs of nests were well repaired. White storks left their nests and migrated to warm countries.

But one raven didn't fix his nest. Nevertheless, he had a feeling that strong winds would blow. Sure enough, the next day strong winds started to blow all over.

As soon as the wind started to blow, the raven's nest was totally destroyed by it. And the raven shouted to the Strong Wind in anger, "This all happened because of you. Are you happy with it now?"

The Strong Wind was very shocked by such an attitude.

"But . . . but . . . ," he tried to explain, but the raven did not want to listen to anything.

The Strong Wind burst into tears and went away from there. When the other winds saw him crying, they asked him what had happened. The Strong Wind told everything to his friends.

So, they tried to calm their friend. "You only did your duty. It is the raven who didn't take measures beforehand, and went wrong. That was his fault, not yours."

Then all the winds went to the raven to have a word with him. The raven understood that is was his fault and apologized to the Strong Wind. In a short time the raven made a safe nest for himself.

The blowing winds pleased people so much, because everyone was cooled down by the pleasant breeze. Clouds were moving in the sky because of the winds.

And whenever the wind would blow, children said this prayer:
"O Allah, how good these clouds are
That clean up everywhere!
They are mild and they are strong.
Please, make them rain whenever we need."

20

WIND GAMES

Hello friends! First, let me introduce myself to you. I am wind. When I blow, you feel me very well, don't you? You cannot see me, but feel me. Sometimes, when I blow hard, you can also hear my sound. Shall I tell you a wind game now?

WIND MACHINE

How about playing this game in a little pond? Then you need a toy sail boat made out of paper. You may ask your parents for help to build this sail boat. Put the sail boat on the water and blow slowly. It is swimming now, isn't it? Now, you can blow with a straw to make it float fast. Like a wind machine. Then, blow with the straw on other objects around you. Let's see what happens.

RAINDROPS

The sky began to get dark early in the morning. The wind came in, and the sky was filled with gray clouds. Pitter patter, pitter patter. Many drops of rain began to fall. The raindrops looked like people parachuting from a plane. God willing, all the raindrops made it down to earth without hitting each other!

Some raindrops said, "Hey! What a beautiful fall from the clouds we have."

"We are landing on soil ever so softly," others said.

Throughout the day, the raindrops fell. Sometimes fast, and sometimes slowly. . .

They fell on trees and flowers, into the oceans, and on animals and human beings.

All the raindrops were very happy, because when rain falls, trees and flowers grow.

But after a while the rain clouds began to slowly disappear.

The very last raindrop had to fall on a dry area, because Allah had given him this task.

The clouds in the sky watched him with curiosity. They wondered where the raindrop would fall.

Suddenly they heard a cry, "I am very thirsty! Again, the drops did not reach me!"

It was a white daisy, weeping.

When the raindrop heard that sound, he said, "Well, I just found what I was looking for. I should immediately fall on that white daisy!"

Then he went quickly down from the sky. Passing amongst the trees, he fell onto the white daisy.

The white daisy was very surprised and excited. "Ah! How nice! Now I feel myself getting very strong, and my leaves are shiny. I will have a long life! Now I will grow very quickly," she said.

Raindrops soaked every place throughout the day. By the will of Allah everyone's needs were met with rain water to grow and to live on. The streets and the roads were washed very clean. Some of the children were playing games jumping in the little ponds.

All living things were saying, "Thank you Allah, for the raindrops you sent us."

The flowers, the trees, the birds, the cats and all the animals were very happy.

The children who love rain said this prayer:
O Allah, how beautiful these raindrops are!
They fall patter-pat, and fill the seas.
They make every place crystal clear. They cheer the plants.
We hope that rain will fall often to bless us.

RAIN GAMES

Hello friends! Let me introduce myself to you. I am a little raindrop. I know how much you love us, the raindrops, because you become very happy when you walk in the rain or when you watch us. Let me tell you a few rain games that I know. Would you like to play along?

LITTLE POND

While it is raining, take a washbowl outside, with your mother's permission, of course. Watch how it fills with water until the rain stops. The raindrops fall one by one, and some circles appear on the surface, don't they? You will see that the raindrops fill the washbowl after a while. When the rain is over, you can play in your little pond, if your mom allows.

The First Game: Take a marble and put it into the water slowly. Do you see the circles? Now, find a flat and thin stick. Put it slowly into the pond. You can see how the waves are getting flat.

The Second Game: You need a rubber duck for this game. First, put your duck into the water. Then, make waves by moving your hand in the water. Your duck is swimming in the pond now, isn't it?

SNOWFLAKES

It was time for sunset. Suddenly, white snowflakes began to fall from the sky.

After a while, the snowflakes lit up the sky.

39

Trees, grasses, houses, cars began to turn white.
Cats, dogs, and birds were looking for their homes.
Through the park could be heard a voice:
"Alas! What am I going to do now? How am I
going to carry all these snowflakes on me?"
This voice was coming from the pine tree.

41

Hearing this, two snowflakes said:

"Calm down! Your shape looks like a triangle. Do you see the roofs of the houses? All the snowflakes do not stay on the roofs. More of them are sliding to the ground. People are constructing the roofs of their houses in the shape of a triangle because they see you in this shape. Do not forget! Almighty Allah gives you this perfect shape.

The small pine tree listened carefully to the snowflakes. One of the snowflakes continued to explain:

"Our shapes are very different from each other. We are sent to the ground to become useful to all living creatures on earth. Sea water increases when we melt. Our water is absorbed by the soil and plants use that water.

46

"Is that so? I did not know that," said the pine tree.

"Yes," the snowflake replied.

Then the pine tree continued:

"Children are very happy when they see you. Some of them make snowmen. Some of them ski."

The snowflakes looked at him and smiled.

The pine tree watched children playing snowballs for a long time.

After a while, the snowflakes decreased. The small pine tree said with excitement:

"Let's go for it! Fall on me! Fall on me!"

"Sure!" the snowflakes said.

Millions of snowflakes were at work. Snowfall continued throughout the night.

In the morning, everywhere was white. There was a white blanket all around. What a pleasure it was to watch the snowflakes! But after a while, the snowflakes stopped falling. Suddenly the sun appeared in the sky. Everyone felt the warmth of the sun.

Then the white blanket began to melt down.

Birds came out of their nests and looked for food.

Children were very eager to see more snow during the winter season. They came together and prayed as follows:

"O Allah, how beautiful are all these snowflakes with all their different shapes. We hope it snows again, as it did last night, and cheers us all up again."

SNOW GAMES

Hello friends! First, let me introduce myself to you. I am a snowflake. I know how much you love us, the snowflakes. Because you are very happy when you watch us and play games, aren't you? I want to tell you two games about snow now. You will have so much fun while playing these games.

MELTING SNOWFLAKES AND ICEBERG

Fill the half of a big glass with water, and the other half with snowflakes. The water begins to overflow when the snowflakes melt, doesn't it? Let's make the melted snowflakes ice now. Fill the plastic molds with the water in the glass. Then put them into the freezer. You will see that the water becomes ice after one hour. Put these ice cubes one on top of each other in a big bowl. Watch how our iceberg melts away.